The Maze

Carla Maney

VANTAGE PRESS
New York

Illustrated by Edgar Blakeney

FIRST EDITION

Copyright © 1995 by Carla Maney

Published by Vantage Press, Inc.
516 West 34th Street, New York, New York 10001

Manufactured in the United States of America
ISBN: 0-533-10152-2

0 9 8 7 6 5 4 3 2 1

The Maze

My name is Jeremy and I am twelve years old. For a long time now I have been looking forward to reaching the age of twelve. Now that I am twelve years old, I can enter the Maze.

I have always found the Maze to be very fascinating. Some people are afraid to enter the Maze. They say it is very dark and gloomy in the Maze and difficult to find your way through it. But I am not afraid to enter the Maze. I think it is an interesting experience, and I think I will find it a challenge.

There are several others who are going to enter the Maze with me. I know one boy. His name is Jacob. I know that Jacob is not twelve years old, and it is a rule that you must be twelve years old. I know for a fact that Jacob is only eleven years old. But it looks like he is going to enter the Maze anyway. That doesn't surprise me because Jacob is always doing things he isn't supposed to do. I think that is why I have never really liked him very much.

The Wizard came through the opening of the Maze. He is a very small man and also a very old man. Some people think that the Wizard is strange, and some people are afraid of him. I just think of him as a wise old man.

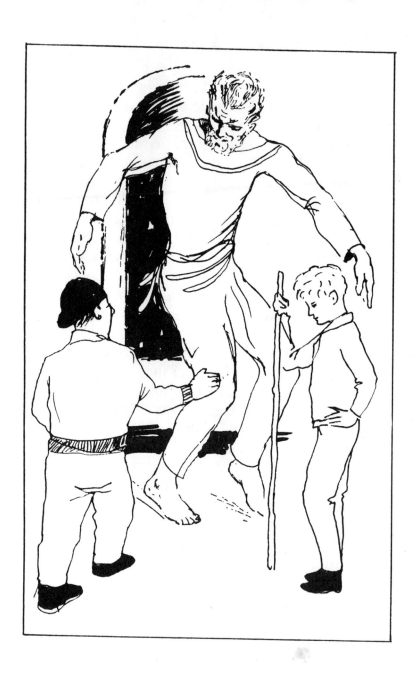

The Wizard spoke slowly in a deep voice, "All young men who wish to enter the Maze, come and gather in front of me."

As we gathered around, Jacob noticed me standing next to him.

"Well, look who is here," said Jacob. "Are you going to enter the Maze, Jeremy?"

"Yes," I answered, "I am going to enter the Maze."

"I really don't think that you will get through the Maze, Jeremy. You just don't have what it takes. Maybe if you stick with me, you might make it."

"Don't worry about me, Jacob. I can take care of myself."

"Now, listen carefully, my sons," said the Wizard. "If you wish to enter the Maze, I have a few rules that you must follow: One, you must be twelve years old. Two, do not bring food into the Maze; you may, however, bring a canteen of water. Three, do not bring any weapons into the Maze. Four, during your journey through the Maze, always be kind to the others who also are going through the Maze. And five, when you come to a door, give it a gentle push. If the door opens, you may go through the doorway. If the door does not open, turn around and find a different path to follow. Never force any doors open.

"Remember these rules, my sons. If you can accomplish the journey through the Maze, there will be a reward waiting there for you."

All the boys began whispering to each other after they heard about the reward. "Hey, Jeremy," said Jacob. "What do you think the reward is?"

"I don't know and I don't care," I replied. "I just want to see if I can make it through the Maze."

"I think the reward is a pot of gold," said Jacob. "I am going to get through that Maze no matter what, and I will be rich from the gold. I will live like a king for the rest of my life."

"You all may now begin your journey through the Maze," announced the Wizard.

The Wizard turned around and entered the Maze. We all entered the Maze right after he did, but he was nowhere to be seen. It was almost as if he had disappeared completely after he entered the Maze.

Everything that I had heard about the Maze proved to be true. It was very dark and gloomy and difficult to find your way around. I looked around at the others and they looked a little afraid, all except for Jacob. Jacob never seems to be afraid of anything.

"Everyone follow me," said Jacob. "We will get through this Maze in no time and find the pot of gold and be rich forever."

Everyone followed Jacob without any hesitation. I don't think it was because they wanted a pot of gold. I think they were a little afraid to go on by themselves. I really don't blame them. I was a little afraid myself.

The Maze was a lot bigger than I had thought it would be. There were several paths that would wind and twist and turn. All the paths were separated by shrubs and brush and a lot of vines. It seemed like we walked for a long time before we came to the first door. Jacob gave it a gentle push and it sprang open.

"That was real easy," said Jacob. "Everyone follow me, and we will get through this Maze in no time at all."

We kept walking on. Before long, we were all beginning to get tired. "Let's stop and rest for a while," said Jacob.

We all sat down and took sips of water from our canteens. Jacob pulled something from his pocket and started eating it. It looked like a piece of meat that was smoked and salt-cured as a preservative. "I was smart enough to bring something to eat to give me more energy," said Jacob. "The rest of you will become weak and tired from hunger, and I will be strong."

I tried to ignore Jacob as much as I could. He was really beginning to annoy me.

We all went on. It was becoming more

difficult to walk because the vines were getting to be very thick. Sometimes they would almost trip you or tangle around your arms. Jacob pulled out a knife from inside his coat and started chopping vines to clear the way. It didn't surprise me that he'd brought a weapon. Breaking rules was Jacob's way of doing things.

We all went on slowly. I noticed Jacob was constantly drinking from his canteen of water. The salty piece of meat he had eaten had probably made him more thirsty than the rest of us, and he soon ran out of water. "Would anyone like to share some of their water with me?" asked Jacob.

"We all need our water for ourselves," I answered. "We could have a long journey ahead of us. You should have sipped on your water slowly like the rest of us."

"That is fine with me," said Jacob. "When I find the pot of gold I will keep it all to myself, and I won't share it with anyone."

As we went on, the path semed to narrow. It was becoming thicker with vines. I heard someone fall and cry out for help.

"Leave him alone," said Jacob. "He has to get through the Maze himself. If we stop to help him, we will never get through the Maze."

"I am going to stop and help him," I said.

"Go right ahead, Jeremy," said Jacob. "You

will never make it through the Maze anyway. Come on, the rest of you. Follow me."

I helped the boy who had fallen. He was all tangled up in the vines, and it wasn't easy to get him untangled. "How did you fall?" I asked. "Did you trip on the vines?"

"No, I didn't trip. Someone grabbed my canteen of water and then pushed me into the vines. I think I twisted my ankle."

"There, now, I have your leg free from the vines," I said. "Can you walk on it?"

"Yes, I can walk, but it is sore. I am going to return to the beginning of the Maze. I don't like the Maze. I am afraid of it."

"Well, that is your choice, but I wish to go on."

We parted and I soon caught up to the others. I could hear their voices. They sat down to take another rest. As I approached them, I noticed Jacob was drinking from a canteen of water. I knew then that he was the one who had pushed the boy into the vines and stolen his canteen.

"Well, look who is here," said Jacob. "I am real surprised to see you, Jeremy. I thought you'd turned around and gone back. Come on, everyone. I don't think it will be much farther."

We all walked on and we soon came to another door. Jacob pushed on the door, but this door would not budge. "Everyone, help me push this door open," said Jacob.

I stood back while all the other boys helped Jacob push on the door, but the door would not budge. "Come and help us, Jeremy," said Jacob.

"No, I will not," I said. "The Wizard said not to force any doors open."

"Oh, who listens to the Wizard; he is just a crazy old man. What does he know, anyway? Stand back, everyone, and I will handle this myself."

Jacob took his knife and pried the door open. As soon as he opened the door, we all heard something crying. It sounded like it was coming from an animal. I started to walk toward the noise and I found a baby unicorn. He was tangled up in the vines.

"We are not stopping to help the unicorn," said Jacob. "We are almost there, and he is just a dumb animal anyway."

"I am going to stop to help the unicorn," I said. "I will then continue my journey through the Maze by myself. I am real tired of the way you do things, Jacob. You broke all of the rules. From now on I am going to make my own decisions."

"That is fine with me, Jeremy. You are really stupid, and you will never make it through the

13

Maze. Come on, everyone, follow me."

They went on without me, and I untangled the unicorn from the vines. His legs were tangled so badly in the vines that it was difficult to get him free. The poor little thing probably would have died there if nobody had helped him.

I finally got him free, and he jumped up and rubbed his head gently against my leg. It seemed like he was trying to say thank you to me. I moved some of the vines out of the way so he wouldn't get tangled up again. After I moved some of the vines, I could see that there was a path there. Nobody had seen the path there earlier because the vines covered it up.

I started to walk down the path, and I noticed that the unicorn was directly behind me. We walked for a little ways till we came to a door. I gave the door a push, but it would not budge. I didn't try to force the door open. I made up my mind that I was going to do things right. We turned and followed a path in a different direction. We soon came to another door. I gave that door a gentle push, and the door sprang right open.

As we walked through the doorway, I noticed that it seemed a little different. It was very cold, dark, and damp, and the path seemed like it started to narrow. I was getting very tired, and things were starting to get a little scary. I looked down at the unicorn, and he also looked a little frightened. I gently patted him on the head. I didn't want him to be afraid. I wanted him to know that I would take care of him and he would be fine.

I decided to sit down and rest for a while because I was really becoming exhausted. I sat down and the unicorn lay down beside me and put his head on my lap. I took a drink of water from my canteen, and I also gave the unicorn a drink in the palm of my hand. He seemed to be very thirsty.

"You sure are lucky that I found you," I said to him. "I'm lucky too that I found you. You are a gentle, loving animal. You mean more to me than any pot of gold. Maybe that is what I will call you. I will call you Lucky. Well, come on, Lucky. Let's be on our way."

We walked on and on. The path was not so narrow anymore, and it was not quite so dark either. It looked as if there was a door not far ahead of us. As I came closer, I could see that it was a double door. I thought that was a little strange because before there had always been only single doors. I put my left hand on one door and my right hand on the other. I gave both doors a gentle push, and they suddenly sprang wide open.

Suddenly there was light shining through the doorway. The light was so bright that it hurt my eyes. I shut my eyes tight and put my arm up over my eyes. Lucky also shut his eyes tight and dropped his head and turned away.

After a short time, our eyes became used to the bright light and we were able to see. We walked through the doorway and there was the most beautiful place I had ever seen in my whole life. There were beautiful trees and green grass and a stream of water trickling down. There were turtles and fish in the water and animals all around on the land. There were squirrels, rabbits, deer, bears, and many beautiful birds. The animals all seemed to be very happy. The whole area seemed to be very peaceful.

"Well, Lucky," I said, "I think we made it through the Maze. I guess you really are lucky for me."

Off in the distance, I could see a cute, little house sitting up on top of a small hill. The house looked like it was well taken care of; it was as neat and tidy as could be. There was a small vegetable garden and beautiful flowers growing all around the house.

I walked over to the stream of water, and Lucky followed right behind me. We had used up all the water in my canteen long ago, and we were very thirsty. I was sure the water was clean because I saw a deer drinking from it. Lucky and I enjoyed the sparkling, fresh water.

After we had drunk our fill, I heard a voice behind me that startled me. "Welcome, Jeremy. I see you made it through the Maze."

I turned around and looked to see who it was, and there was the wise old Wizard. *He must be the one who lives in the little house up on top of the hill,* I thought. "Yes, I guess I did make it through the Maze. I guess I was lucky."

"No, my son, it was not luck that got you through the Maze," said the Wizard with a smile. "You got through the Maze because you made good decisions and the right choices. Because you were able to make good choices, you found the right path, and that is how you accomplished the journey through the Maze."

"Did Jacob make it through the Maze?"

"He certainly did not," answered the Wizard with a frown. "He broke all of the rules. He thought that he could make it through the Maze by lying, cheating, and stealing. Well, he is very wrong. No one will make it through the Maze with an attitude like that."

"Did the other boys make it through the Maze? They did not lie, cheat, steal, or break all of the rules."

"No, my son, the others did not make it through the Maze either. Maybe they didn't lie, cheat, steal, or break all of the rules, but they did choose to follow the wrong person. In order for them to get through the Maze, they will have to make good choices and the right decisions. Before anyone can make good choices and the right decisions, they first must be able to make up their own minds about things. No one person will make it through the Maze by following in the same footsteps as the person before him."

"Mr. Wizard, what is the reward? Jacob thinks that it is a pot of gold."

"Jacob's way of thinking is wrong. I never said that the reward was a pot of gold. There are many things in life that are much more rewarding. Tell me something, Jeremy. Do you feel good about yourself because you accomplished your journey through the Maze?"

"Yes, I do. I feel very good about myself."

"Then that is your reward. There is never a more rewarding feeling than when a person accomplishes something by going about it in the right way. That is what builds good, strong character. A person with a good, strong character is a good person and will probably be a success at anything he does. Now, my son, you have a much bigger journey ahead of you."

"What journey is that, Mr. Wizard?"

"You now have the journey of your whole life ahead of you. Treat your journey through life the same way you treated your journey through the Maze. Handle each problem as it is

set before you in the best way that you can. Try always to use good judgement and make good decisions and the right choices. Do what you feel is right in your heart. If you do this, you will always follow the right path and you will always go in the right direction. Now, be on your way, young man. You have your whole life ahead of you."

"What should I do with the unicorn?"

"Take the unicorn with you. Keep him with you always. Because of your kindness, he feels you are his very best friend."

"Good-bye, Mr. Wizard. I learned a lot from you today."

"No, my son. You learned a lot from yourself today. You will continue to learn a lot from yourself on each day ahead of you. Follow the path ahead of you, and it will lead you to the village."

Lucky and I walked down the path, and I could see the village off in the distance. As I walked along, I thought about what the Wizard had said to me. The Wizard was right. It was a very rewarding feeling to have accomplished the journey through the Maze, and I did feel good about myself. It made me feel like I was not afraid of anything. *Whenever I am faced with any problem,* I thought, *I will try to make the right decision and handle it the best way I can.*

Some people think that the Wizard is strange and has magical powers, and some people are afraid of him. I don't think he is strange or has magical powers, and I am not afraid of him at all. I think he is a good friend, and he is a person like everyone else. The only thing that is a little different about him is that he got to be very old and very wise. I hope I will be just like him someday.